Sweet Dreams,
Little One

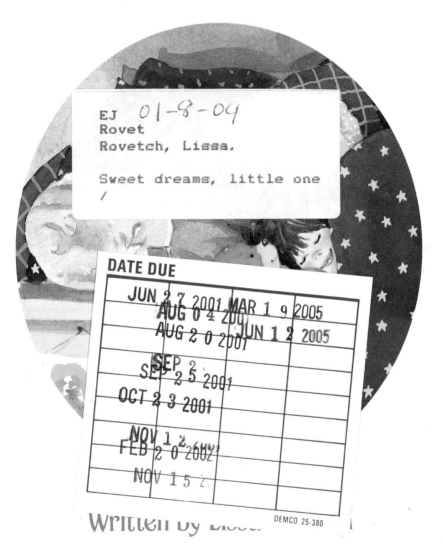

Written by Lissa

Illustrated by Betina Ogden

a KNEE-HIGH book®

Random House 🏠 New York

"Sweet dreams, Little One,"
said Mama.

"But, Mama," said Little One,
"I'm all out of dreams."

"In that case," said Mama,
"we'll just have to come up with
some new ones."

"Mama," said Little One,
"what do you think animal
mamas tell their little ones to
dream about?"

"Close your eyes, Little One,"
said Mama. "Close your eyes
and I will tell you."

Cat Dream

Dream about string
to tangle and chase.
Dream about catnip
all over the place.
Dream about ponds
with plenty of fish.
Dream about cream
in a bottomless dish.

Horse Dream

Dream about running
through fields of flowers.
Dream about playing in
silver spring showers.
Dream about rainbows
that glow in the sky.
Dream about butterflies
fluttering by.

Squirrel Dream

Dream of the games
that you play by the creek.
Dream about freeze tag
and hide-and-go-seek.
Dream that you climb
to the top of the tree,
then dream that you scamper
straight back here to me.

Fish Dream

Dream about stars
that shine in the sea.
Dream about swimming
happy and free.
Dream about drifting
in oceans of blue.
Dream about fishy friends
playing with you.

Rabbit Dream

Dream about carrots
piled so high.
Dream about jumping
straight up to the sky.
Dream about digging
a burrow so deep.
Sweet dreams, little bunny.
Hush now, go to sleep.

Eagle Dream

Dream about floating
on clouds of warm air.
Dream about soaring
around everywhere.
Dream about canyons
and deserts and streams.
Dream about flying
through golden moonbeams.

Bear Dream

Dream about snow
falling gently out there.
Dream about hugging
your big mama bear.
Dream about being
so mighty and brave.
Dream all night long
in our safe, cozy cave.

Otter Dream

*Dream about waves
splashing up, splashing down.
Dream that you're wearing
a fine seashell crown.
Dream of soft seaweed
under your head.
Dream as you sleep
in your watery bed.*

Little One's Dream

Dream about fish
that swim in the sea.
Dream about birds
that fly wild and free.
Dream about animals
snuggled up tight.
Sweet dreams, Little One.
Sweet dreams and good night.